MUSH,

A DOG FROM Space

Pinkwater's guides to the galaxy

Borgel

Guys from Space

Spaceburger

Ned Feldman, Space Pirate

MUSH,
A Dog From Space

BY DANIEL PINKWATER
ILLUSTRATED BY JILL PINKWATER

Aladdin
New York   London   Toronto   Sydney   Singapore

TO Arctic Flake and Jill

First edition July 2002

Text copyright © 1995 by Daniel Pinkwater
Illustrations copyright © 2002 by Jill Pinkwater

ALADDIN PAPERBACKS
An imprint of Simon & Schuster Children's Publishing Division
1230 Avenue of the Americas, New York, New York 10020

Designed by Lisa Vega
The text of this book was set in Cheltenham Book
Printed in the United States of America
2 4 6 8 10 9 7 5 3 1

Library of Congress Cataloging-in-Publication Data

Pinkwater, Daniel Manus, 1941-
Mush, a dog from space / by Daniel Pinkwater ; illustrated by Jill Pinkwater.
p. cm.
Summary: Kelly, who has wanted a pet dog for a long time, runs into a
highly-educated, mushamute dog from the planet Growf-Woof-Woof.
ISBN 0-689-84800-5—ISBN 0-689-84801-3
[1. Pets—Fiction. 2. Dogs—Fiction. 3. Extraterrestrial beings—Fiction.]
I. Pinkwater, Jill, ill. II. Title.
PZ7.P6335 Mus 2002
[Fic]—dc21
2002004422

Contents

The New House

I am Kelly Mangiaro. I am a kid. I used to live in an apartment with my mother and father, and no pets. That was a rule in the apartment house: No Pets.

But not long ago, we moved to a brand-new house. It is in a brand-new development. A development is a place where lots of brand-new houses are built all at once. All the other houses have people in them who used to live in apartments. The development is in the middle

of the woods, near a town. It is not finished yet. They are still building some of the brand-new houses.

Now that we were living in our own house, there was no rule about No Pets. I told my mother and father that I expected to have a dog, or at least a cat, soon.

My parents had a new reason for No Pets. They said it was too soon for a pet. They said that it would take some time to get settled in the new house. They said that maybe I could have a pet when the new furniture didn't look so new anymore.

"You mean, I can't have a dog or anything until this place stops being perfect?" I asked them.

They said it was something like that.

Bummer.

The Woods

All the people in the other brand-new houses had babies and kids a little older than babies. I could make lots of money baby-sitting, but there were no kids my age or even near my age. I was getting rich, but I had no friends. My mother said that would change when school started. I saved my baby-sitting money. I could use it to buy a dog when the time came.

I spent a lot of time alone, walking in the

woods. I liked the woods. I had never spent time in real woods before. When we lived in the apartment, I would go to the park—but that was very different. The woods were wild, and if I was quiet, I could get close to lots of birds and animals. Sometimes I would see the footprints of deer, but I never saw one.

I would always take a sandwich, and something to drink, and my compass, and a notebook to write down the kinds of birds and animals I saw. It would have been better if I had a friend with me on my walks in the woods—or a dog.

My Mother Gets a Job

efore I was born, my mother used to work in an office. Now she decided to go to work again. She said the extra money would help us get more brand-new, perfect furniture sooner. My father and mother talked about it. They said they could not leave me home alone while they both worked all day. I said it would be all right to leave me at home. They decided they would find someone to stay with me. I did not like the idea. I was a baby-sitter myself—I did not need a baby-sitter. "It is undignified," I said.

My mother found a job in the office of a company that makes frozen chicken dinners—and she found a lady to stay with me, Mrs. Brillo. Mrs. Brillo wore funny-smelling perfume like wilted flowers. All day, she sat in the brand-new rocking chair, reading the newspaper. At 11:55 in the morning, she would jump up and put two frozen chicken dinners in the brand-new microwave. The frozen chicken dinner company had given my mother a big box of frozen chicken dinners on her first day at work.

Mrs. Brillo and I would eat our frozen chicken dinners. Then she would recycle the plastic plates, wash the knives and forks, and go back to reading the newspaper. Mrs. Brillo was a nice lady, I suppose—but she was boring. And I did not like the idea of having a baby-sitter.

Something Strange in the Woods

One day, while Mrs. Brillo was reading her newspaper, after we had eaten our frozen chicken dinners for lunch, I was walking in the woods. I saw a rabbit. I stood very still. So did the rabbit. I watched it for a long time. Then the rabbit sort of forgot I was there, and began to eat grass. I knew that as long as I stayed perfectly still, the rabbit would not be frightened, and would not go away. I tried not to move a muscle. I tried to breathe as softly as I could. It was very quiet in the woods. Bright sun was shining through the leaves. There was no wind. The rabbit was beautiful, and I was close enough to see every whisker.

Then, something strange happened. I knew I was not alone. I don't know how I knew it, but there was something watching me— something big. It was watching me, not moving, breathing softly, just the way I was watching the rabbit.

I was not scared. I was curious. Slowly, slowly, I turned my head to see whatever was watching me. "It could be a bear," I thought. But I was not scared.

At first, I did not see anything. Then, I saw ears. There were two ears, sticking up from behind some bushes. They were big—but they did not look like bear's ears.

"Hello, animal," I said.

The rabbit hopped away.

The ears twitched.

"I am not scared," I said. "Don't you be scared."

I reached into my pocket. There was an oatmeal cookie.

"Oh, good!" I thought.

I held out the cookie. "Do you want this cookie, animal?" I asked.

The bushes moved. The animal was coming out. I put the cookie on the ground, and took a step or two backward. I was not scared—just cautious.

It was a dog! A really big dog! I could tell right away the dog was friendly. It was black and white and gray. The dog sniffed the cookie.

"You may have the cookie," I said to the dog.

"Thank you," the dog said. "It isn't your last one, is it? I wouldn't want to eat your last cookie."

"It's okay," I said. "I'm not hungry. I just had a frozen chicken dinner. Please eat the cookie."

"Well, if you insist," the dog said.

It ate the cookie.

"Hey!" I said.

"What?" the dog said.

"I just realized. You can talk!"

"So can you," the dog said. "What's so special about that?"

"It's unusual," I said.

"If you say so," said the dog. "Do you live around here?"

"I live in a brand-new house," I said. "Do you live around here?"

"Not really," the dog said.

"Is your home far away?"

"My home is very far away," the dog said.

"My name is Kelly," I said.

"My name is Mush," the dog said.

By now, I had gotten closer to the dog, and I was stroking its thick fur. The dog was sort of leaning against me.

"What kind of dog are you?" I asked.

"I am a mushamute," Mush said.

"I've never heard of that kind of dog."

"I'm not surprised," Mush said.

"Well, you are a good boy," I said, scratching Mush between the ears.

"I'm a good girl," said Mush.

Mush

Mush looked like one of those dogs that pulls sleds in Alaska—sort of like a fat wolf.

"Are you a husky?" I asked Mush.

"I am a mushamute," Mush said. "I am certainly the only mushamute on this planet."

"How can that be?" I asked. "Your mother and father must have been mushamutes."

"That is so," said Mush.

"And you have brothers and sisters?"

"Many."

"Then how could you be the only mushamute on this planet?" I asked.

"Guess," Mush said.

"Did something terrible happen to your mother and father, and all the other mushamutes?" I asked.

"No," said Mush.

"And yet, you are the only mushamute on this planet."

"That is correct," Mush said.

I thought for a while. "Are there mushamutes on some planet other than Earth?"

"Yes, there are," Mush said.

"Are you from another planet?"

"You guessed it!" Mush said. "I come from a planet known as Growf-Woof-Woof, in the solar system of Arfturus, a star similar to Canis Major in your galaxy."

"You are a dog from space?"

"Yes."

"Wow! That means you don't belong to anybody on Earth!"

"I suppose you could say that," Mush said.

"So you could come and live with me," I said. "That is, if you would like to."

"We could give it a try," Mush said.

By this time, Mush and I were walking together through the woods in the direction of my house.

"Is that the reason you are able to talk to me—because you are a dog from another planet?" I asked.

"I am able to talk to you because I am a highly educated dog," Mush said.

We walked a little farther.

"Did you know that 'Mush!' is what sled-dog drivers say to make their dogs go?" I asked.

"Yes, I knew that," Mush said.

We walked on.

"Does it ever snow here?" Mush asked.

"Oh, yes—in the winter," I said.

"Good," Mush said.

We walked some more.

"How did you happen to come to Earth?" I asked.

"It's a long story," said Mush.

Little by Little

I thought it would be good to get my mother and father used to the idea of Mush living with us little by little.

"Look, Mush," I said. "I think you should stay in the garage at first."

"What's the garage?" Mush asked.

"It's a place where they keep the car, only they never put the car in it, because they don't want to get it dirty. There is a door from the garage to the house, and when they are busy, or asleep, I can sneak you inside."

"Why sneak? Don't your mother and father like dogs?"

"It's just that they are worried about the house getting dirty," I said.

"So?" Mush asked. "What has that got to do with me? I am a very tidy dog."

"Just do it my way," I said. "When they do find out about you, I can tell them that you've already been living with us, and you are so little trouble they didn't even know it."

"I don't know. . . ." said Mush.

"Please," I said. "They are good parents. It just takes them a while to understand things."

"Wmmph," said Mush.

In the Kitchen

I spent the rest of the afternoon fixing up a nice place for Mush in the garage. Mrs. Brillo went home at five. My parents didn't get home until six. That gave me an hour to fix Mush some supper. I invited her into the kitchen.

"I don't have any kibble," I said. "I can get some tomorrow."

"What's kibble?" Mush asked.

"Dog food—it comes in a bag. You pour

some out, and mix it with water. Then you eat it out of a bowl."

"It sounds disgusting," Mush said.

"Well, what would you like to eat?" I asked. "I can make you a frozen chicken dinner."

"That doesn't appeal to me either," Mush said. "Do you mind if I just look around for myself?"

Mush opened cupboards, and the refrigerator. It was surprising to see how she was able to handle things with her paws and nose.

I sat on the high kitchen stool, and watched. Mush opened a drawer and removed a sharp knife. Then she sliced a tomato! She peeled some leaves off a head of lettuce, and put the lettuce back in the refrigerator! I was more than surprised. I was amazed!

I was more than amazed when she put two slices of bread in the toaster, opened a jar of peanut butter, and spread it on her

toast with a knife. After she ate her sandwich, she swept up the crumbs, and washed everything she had used.

"That is incredible!" I said.

"What, a peanut butter, lettuce, and tomato sandwich on toast?" Mush asked. "You must not know very much about cooking, if that impresses you. Sometime, I will teach you to prepare a roast duck with all the trimmings. But now, I had better go to the garage. Your mother and father will be home any minute."

"Can you tell that because of your dog instincts?" I asked.

"I can tell that because the kitchen clock says it's five minutes to six," Mush said.

Getting Them Ready

"**W**e didn't have a chance to go to the market," my mother said. "I hope you won't mind frozen chicken dinners tonight."

"Do you know how to cook roast duck with all the trimmings?" I asked.

"We're just a little disorganized, dear," my father said. "Everything will be normal soon."

While we were eating our frozen chicken dinners, I said, "I have decided what kind of dog I want—a mushamute."

"I don't believe I have ever heard of that kind of dog," my mother said.

"They are very rare," I said.

"Dear, do you think you would be all right by yourself tomorrow?" my mother asked.

"Of course," I said.

"Mrs. Brillo left a note," my mother said. "She has quit her job as your baby-sitter. She is going to Colorado to work in a gold mine. I am very disappointed in her."

"I'll be fine," I said.

"And you can fix your own lunch?" my mother asked. "It's very simple. You just put a frozen chicken dinner in the microwave."

"Lunch will not be a problem," I said.

"We will look for another baby-sitter," my father said.

"It may take some time. It was not easy to find Mrs. Brillo."

"You know, I really do not need a baby-sitter," I said.

"We know you feel that way," my mother said. "It is really for our peace of mind. We want to know that you are safe."

"I would be safe if I had a big dog to stay

home with me," I said. "Like a mushamute, for example. They are quite large."

"It would be cheaper than a baby-sitter," my father said. "All a dog needs is a bag of kibble."

"Or some kind of food," I said. "Mushamutes don't care for kibble."

"Of course, the dog would have to be well trained," my mother said.

"Mushamutes are highly educated," I said.

"Well, we will think about it," my father said. "Meanwhile, we will look for a baby-sitter."

It was hard work, but I had gotten the idea into their heads.

On Our Own

I had breakfast with my mother and father. Mush had a doughnut and a cup of coffee after they left for work. "I've never been a breakfast sort of dog," she said.

We spent most of the morning in the woods. Mush was able to notice all sorts of things I had never noticed. "There's a fox in these woods," she said.

"There is? How can you tell?" I asked.

"Oh, you can smell it, plain as day. Foxes stink."

I sniffed. "I don't smell anything special," I said.

"Sniff again," Mush said. "Close your eyes when you sniff."

"It just smells like the woods," I said.

"You are smelling everything all at once. Smell the smells one at a time," Mush said.

I tried. "That's grass," I said. "That's moss. That's some kind of flower. That's tree bark. And ... ugh! What is that?"

"That's the fox," Mush said. "Nasty, isn't he?"

"That's how a fox smells?" I asked.

"Yes," Mush said. "Want to see him? Hey, fox! Come out and show yourself!"

When Mush called the fox, I heard her in my head. I was able to understand what she was saying to the fox. What my ears heard was a sort of whine—almost like a whistle.

Then I heard a rough, raspy sound, coming from somewhere nearby. "Oh, no I won't!" I heard in my head. "You'll tear me to bits, you horrible big dog."

"I will do no such thing, and you know it," Mush was telling the fox. "If I even touched you, I'd have to take five baths."

"This is unbelievable!" I said. "I can understand what you and the fox are saying to each other! How can this be?"

"You must be a special kid," Mush said to me — and to the fox she said, "Are you going to come out, or do I drag you out?"

The fox came out of the bushes. It was so beautiful it almost hurt my eyes. Its fur was a bright orange red like nothing I had ever seen. Its pointy nose and tiny feet were so perfect, and its bushy tail was carried so proudly, it seemed like the king of animals, even more wonderful than Mush.

"However," Mush said, guessing, or hearing, what I was thinking, "it smells like stale fish."

"Have you had a good look?" the fox said. "I have things to do, you know."

"Yes, thank you," Mush said. "And take a bath."

"Go chase your tail, you big pussycat," the

fox said, and disappeared into the under-brush.

"Foxes are all like that," Mush said. "Too smart for their own good."

"This is great!" I said. "Show me some more!"

"Tomorrow," Mush said. "We have to go home and fix lunch now."

A New Way of Doing Things

Lunch was Spanish omelets and home-fried potatoes, prepared by Mush—with me peeling and slicing the potatoes. Mush showed me how.

"Are we going back to the woods?" I asked Mush after she had washed the dishes. I dried.

"Have you got any money?" Mush asked.

"I have lots of money. I made it baby-sitting," I told her.

"Get your money," Mush said. "I think we

should hike into town and buy a few things."

"Like what?" I asked.

"Like groceries," Mush said. "You are going to cook supper tonight."

"I am?"

"You are. And I am going to help you. But first, come into the garage and help me. I don't know why, but I've never been any good with knots."

In the garage, Mush had found my old red wagon, and some clothesline. She had me tie the clothesline to the wagon, making a sort of loop, and a short piece of clothesline from one side of the loop to the other, making a big letter A.

"Now, toss the clothesline into the wagon. You can pull it by the handle on the way there," Mush said.

"You know, they aren't going to allow you inside the market," I said.

"Why not?" Mush asked.

"No dogs. It's a rule," I said.

"What a silly rule," Mush said. "Well, I will wait outside with the wagon. On the way to town, I will tell you what to buy and you can write it down in your notebook."

"I was hoping that on the way to town, you would tell me how you happened to leave your planet and come to Earth," I said.

"I'll tell you another time," Mush said. "Now let's get started."

Roast Duck With All the Trimmings

It was a long list. I came out of the market with three full bags in my shopping cart. I put them in the wagon. Then I helped Mush get the clothesline arranged, with the loop around her chest, and the short piece of clothesline across her back. She pulled the wagon, and I walked alongside and helped steer.

When we got home, we got busy in the kitchen. Mush told me what to do, and I did it. It was fun slicing and mashing and mixing and cooking. Mush kept looking at the clock. Everything had to be ready at the same time—the roast duck, the salad, the three kinds of vegetables, the hot rolls, and the apple pie. We used every brand-new appliance in the brand-new kitchen. We spent the last hour cleaning up the kitchen and setting the table.

"It's almost six o'clock," Mush said. "I'll just slip into the garage now. You did a very good job, Kelly."

I met my parents at the door.

"The parking lot was just jammed at the market," my mother said. "And your father and I are so tired. I'm afraid it will be frozen chicken dinners again. I do apologize."

"No problem," I said. "Supper will be served in five minutes."

I have never had so much fun in my life as I did looking at my parent's faces when I brought out the steaming bowls of food, and the roast duck.

"You cooked all this?" my father asked. His eyes were big and round.

"Yes," I said.

"But this is roast duck with all the trimmings!" my mother said.

"And there's apple pie for dessert. It's just cooling," I said.

"And you . . . ?"

"I."

"But . . ."

"Eat your food. It's getting cold," I said.

"I don't understand," my father said. Then he said, "This is delicious."

"Yes, it certainly is," my mother said. "But, Kelly dear, do you mean that all by yourself you . . . ?"

"Oh! I forgot the hot rolls!" I said. "I'll be right back."

All through the meal, my parents ate with
such bewildered expressions. A few times, I
had to run into the kitchen and stuff a dish
towel in my mouth so they wouldn't hear me

laughing. In my head, I heard Mush laughing in the garage. By the time I served them their fresh-brewed coffee and apple pie, they had pulled themselves together.

"Now, Kelly," my father said. "This was a wonderful meal and a wonderful surprise, but we had no idea you knew how to cook."

"I'm just learning," I said.

"We are very impressed," my mother said. "But it's hard to believe a girl of your age could do this so . . . perfectly without any help."

"Well, maybe my new baby-sitter helped me," I said.

"But you don't have a baby-sitter," my mother said.

"Then I must have done it by myself," I said.

"I think she's making a point," my mother said to my father.

"Yes, I think she is," my father said to my mother.

"She is very capable," my mother said.

"Still, there's the question of security. It is unwise to leave a child alone these days," my father said. "There are burglars."

"And fiends," my mother said.

"Fire could break out."

"Violent thunderstorms."

"Flash floods."

"And earthquakes happen everywhere."

"Then there are people who come to the door and try to convert you to strange religions."

"Very true."

"Just because a child is able to prepare roast duck with all the trimmings is no reason to leave her unprotected."

"Still, it was a very good meal."

"It was that."

Meeting Mush

While my parents were discussing things, I was in the kitchen, clearing up the supper things, and putting together a big plate of leftovers for Mush. Apparently, my father had gotten up and was walking around—and for some reason, he had opened the door to the garage, because I heard him say, "Hey! There's a big dog in our garage."

I raced to the garage. There was Mush, sitting and looking at my father with a friendly, stupid expression, and wagging her tail. I realized that I had never seen her do that.

"How did this dog get in here?" my father asked. "It looks like a husky."

"It's a mushamute," I said.

My mother had arrived. "So that's a mushamute!" she said. "It's very pretty."

"Kelly, whose dog is this?" my father asked.

"Her name is Mush," I said.

"And . . . ?"

"She's our dog," I said.

"Is she housebroken?" my mother asked.

Mush rolled her eyes. I heard her think, "How much can I stand of this?" But she kept wagging.

"She is perfect, Mom," I said. "She can protect me when you're not home. Mush, speak!"

"Woof!" Mush said. She actually said the word "woof." She forgot to bark—but my parents didn't notice.

"Watch it," I whispered.

"Sorry," I heard Mush think.

"Mush, show your teeth!"

Mush grinned. It was grotesque.

"Mush! Protect me from the bad man!"

Mush sprang to a position between me and my father, and growled. This time, she actually growled like a regular dog. I was afraid she'd say, "Grrrr!"

"This would be better if we'd had time to practice," I thought.

"Call her off!" my father shouted.

"Okay, Mush! He's a good daddy."

Mush went over and licked his hand. I heard her thinking, "This is the last time I do this, buster."

"Mush! Dial the Fire Department!"

Mush bounded for the phone, and knocked it off the hook. Then she punched some buttons, and barked into the receiver. "This is too silly for words," I heard her think.

My father grabbed the receiver, and slammed it down. "Hey! It's impolite to dial people at random and bark at them!" he said.

The phone rang. My father answered. It was the Fire Department wanting to know if we had just called them. "Sorry. It was the dog," my father said. "Yes, I am aware that it is against the law to turn in a false alarm. It was the dog, as I told you. The dog was just fooling around. I'm sorry."

I wasn't done yet. I flopped on the floor. "Mush! I'm overcome!" Mush grabbed the leg of my jeans and dragged me out the front door onto the lawn, and barked for help. My parents were applauding by now.

"I've got one more! Okay, Mush! I'm choking on a frozen chicken dinner!"

This was a mistake. Mush flew at me and hit me in the stomach with all four paws, hard enough to dislodge any chicken dinner I might have been choking on—and really almost, the duck dinner I had just eaten.

"Oof!" I gasped.

"Serves you right," Mush thought audibly. "Big show-off!"

"She certainly is well trained," my mother said.

"As I told you, mushamutes are highly educated," I said.

In the Clear

It was a done deal. Mush was staying. She moved from the garage into my room that very night. She was curled up on the rug, and I was tucked up in bed.

"I hope you will like living with us," I said.

"Oh, yes. It will be lots of fun," Mush said.

"Will you ever tell me about how you came to Earth?" I asked.

"Yes," Mush said. "But not tonight. It's getting late."

I thought she sounded a little sad. "Do you miss your home planet?" I asked.

"I miss some things," Mush said. "For instance, I used to have a pet."

"Was your pet a little girl?" I asked.

"How did you guess?" Mush asked.

"I don't know—just guessed," I said.

"Well, it's time to get some sleep," Mush said. "Lots to do tomorrow."

Ready-for-Chapters

Enjoy the very best first chapter book fiction in Ready-for-Chapters books from Aladdin Paperbacks.

☐ **Jake Drake, Bully Buster**
by Andrew Clements

☐ **Annabel the Actress Starring in Gorilla My Dreams**
by Ellen Conford

☐ **The Bears on Hemlock Mountain**
by Alice Dalgliesh

☐ **The Courage of Sarah Noble**
by Alice Dalgliesh

☐ **The Girl with 500 Middle Names**
by Margaret Peterson Haddix

☐ **The Werewolf Club**
#1 The Magic Pretzel
by Daniel Pinkwater

☐ **The Werewolf Club**
#2 The Lunchroom of Doom
by Daniel Pinkwater

☐ **The Werewolf Club**
#3 The Werewolf Club Meets Dorkula
by Daniel Pinkwater

☐ **The Cobble Street Cousins**
#1 In Aunt Lucy's Kitchen
by Cynthia Rylant

☐ **The Cobble Street Cousins**
#2 A Little Shopping
by Cynthia Rylant

☐ **The Cobble Street Cousins**
#3 Special Gifts
by Cynthia Rylant

☐ **Third-Grade Detectives**
#1 The Clue of the Left-Handed Envelope
by George Edward Stanley

☐ **Third-Grade Detectives**
#2 The Puzzle of the Pretty Pink Handkerchief
by George Edward Stanley

☐ **Third-Grade Detectives**
#3 The Mystery of the Hairy Tomatoes
by George Edward Stanley

Everyone needs Puppy Friends™!

Bouncy and cute, furry and huggable, what could be more perfect than a puppy?

by
Jenny Dale

#1 Gus the Greedy Puppy
0-689-83423-3 $3.99

#2 Lily the Lost Puppy
0-689-83404-7 $3.99

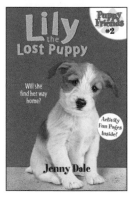

#3 Spot the Sporty Puppy
0-689-83424-1 $3.99

#4 Lenny the Lazy Puppy
0-689-83552-3 $3.99

#5 Max the Muddy Puppy
0-689-83553-1 $3.99

#6 Billy the Brave Puppy
0-689-83554-X $3.99

#7 Nipper the Noisy Puppy
0-689-83974-X $3.99

ALADDIN PAPERBACKS
Simon & Schuster Children's Publishing
www.SimonSaysKids.com